Translated by Ineke Lenting

First published in the United States and Canada in 2016
by Lemniscaat USA LLC • New York
Distributed in the United States by Ingram Publisher Services

First U.S. edition 2016

Library of Congress Cataloging-in-Publication Data
Veldkamp, Tjibbe.
Sam and the Construction Site / by Tjibbe Veldkamp;
Illustrated by Alice Hoogstad; translated by Ineke Lenting
p.; color illustrations; cm.

ISBN 978-1-935954-49-1 (hardcover)

1. Construction equipment — Juvenile Fiction. 2. Cranes — Juvenile Literature

PZ7 [E]

Printing and binding: Worzalla, Stevens Point, WI USA

TJIBBE VELDKAMP &
ALICE HOOGSTAD

Sam and the Construction Site

LEMNISCAAT

Sam liked the construction site. Every day, he stood behind the fence and studied the big machines—the steamroller, the cement truck, and the crane.
"What if I could drive those machines?" he thought.

The construction workers ate their lunch every day at noon in the office. The boss said, "Sam, no one is allowed to enter the construction site. Will you keep an eye on it?"

"All right," Sam said.

"And if anyone does enter the site, call the police!"

"All right," Sam said.

While the builders were having lunch one day,
a couple of big boys came along.

"Hi there, little guy," the biggest boy said.
"We're not afraid to enter the construction site,
but you're too chicken."

"I'm not," Sam said. "But it's against the rules."

"No, you're too chicken!" the big boys said. "You're afraid!"

"All right," Sam said. "I'll go in, but then you must call the police."

"It's a deal!" the big boys said.

Sam crawled under the fence and walked up to the steamroller.

The biggest boy immediately called the police.

"Officer!" he said. "A little boy is playing on the building site. He's climbing into the steamroller!"

"That's against the rules!" the officer said on the telephone. "We'll be there in a minute!"

"Let's see if I can drive the steamroller," Sam said. He started the engine. First, he flattened the fence and then a car.

The big boys were in shock.

Sam climbed off the steamroller.
He waved at the big boys.

"Now I'm going to go into the cement truck," he said.

"Don't!" the big boys yelled.
"You've just flattened a fence and a car!
There'll be even more accidents!"

But Sam was already behind the wheel.
"Let's see if I can drive the cement truck," he said.

He started the engine, drove a few yards,
and poured concrete onto the road.

"Oh no!" the big boys groaned. "Is that kid crazy?"

Sam got out of the cement truck.
Again he waved at the big boys.
"Now I'll try the crane," he said.

"Don't!" the big boys shouted. "You have just flattened the fence
and a car, and you have poured concrete onto the street! How
many more accidents do you want to cause?"

But Sam was already climbing into the crane.

He sat down in the
crane driver's seat.
"Let's see if I can work
the boom," he said.

He started the engine, made the boom swing around,
and hoisted a police car up into the air.

The builders saw it from inside their office. They ran out
the door and shouted, "Sam! Get out of that crane!"

"Yes!" the big boys shouted. "Sam, get out of that crane!"

"NO!" the policemen in the police car shouted.
"First put us down, Sam, and THEN get out of that crane!"

Sam put the police car down on the ground.
The officers got out and asked, "What's going on here?"

"We haven't done anything wrong!" the big boys squeaked.
"We only said that he was too chicken to enter the
construction site! We didn't know that he would cause all
those accidents!"

"Is that correct?" the policemen asked Sam.

"Yes," Sam said. "I saw a couple of thieves robbing the bank, so I flattened their getaway car. Next, I poured some concrete so that they would get stuck. And when I saw that the drawbridge had opened, I hoisted you up so you would not drive into the river."

Sure enough, there were the two bankrobbers, stuck in the concrete.

At that moment the bank manager ran out of the bank and shouted, "Stop, thieves! Call the police!"

"All taken care of," Sam said.

The policemen borrowed a jackhammer from the builders.
They jackhammered the robbers out of the concrete.

"Thanks, Sam!" the bank manager said. "You have caught
the robbers! How can I reward you?"

"We have an idea!" the builders said.

The bank manager gave Sam a hard-hat.
With the hard-hat on his head,
Sam could enter the building site whenever he wanted.

JUL 1 - 2016